1/22

P9-DWG-705

D0037731

For Amit

Copyright © 2021 by Katie Yamasaki

All rights reserved
Printed in China
First Edition

For information about permission to reproduce selections from this book, write to
Permissions, W. W. Norton & Company, Inc., 500 Fifth Avenue, New York, NY 10110

For information about special discounts for bulk purchases, please contact W. W. Norton
Special Sales at specialsales@wwnorton.com or 800-233-4830

Manufacturing by Toppan Leefung
Book design by Hana Anouk Nakamura
Production manager: Julia Druskin

Library of Congress Cataloging-in-Publication Data
Names: Yamasaki, Katie, author, illustrator.
Title: Dad bakes / Katie Yamasaki.
Description: First edition. | New York : Norton Young Readers, [2021] |
Audience: Ages 4–8 | Summary: Dad rises before the sun, goes to work at the bakery where he kneads,
rolls, and bakes bread, and as the world starts its day, Dad heads home to his young daughter
where they play, read, and bake together.
Identifiers: LCCN 2021007077 | ISBN 9781324015413 (hardcover) | ISBN 9781324015420 (epub)
Subjects: CYAC: Fathers and daughters—Fiction. | Baking—Fiction.
Classification: LCC PZ7.Y19157 Dad 2021 | DDC [E—dc23
LC Record available at https://lccn.loc.gov/2021007077

W. W. Norton & Company, Inc., 500 Fifth Avenue, New York, N.Y. 10110
www.wwnorton.com

W. W. Norton & Company Ltd., 15 Carlisle Street, London W1D 3BS

2 4 6 8 0 9 7 5 3 1

DAD BAKES

Katie Yamasaki

Norton Young Readers
An Imprint of W. W. Norton & Company • Independent Publishers Since 1923

Dad wakes.

The moon shines.

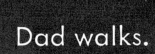

Dad walks.

The sun hides.

Dad arrives.

Working side by side, Dad bakes.

He scoops.
He kneads.
He rolls.

Dough rises.

Dad makes small rolls,
Dad makes large loaves.

The sun rises.

Dad walks.

He smells like
warm bread.

Dad rests.

I wait.

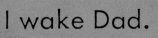

I wake Dad.

We go to the kitchen.

We mix,

we roll.

we knead,

We wait.

And we wait.

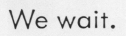

I peek.

"Shhh," Dad says.
"The bread needs peace."

We wait.

And we wait.

And we wait.

Dad rolls the dough.

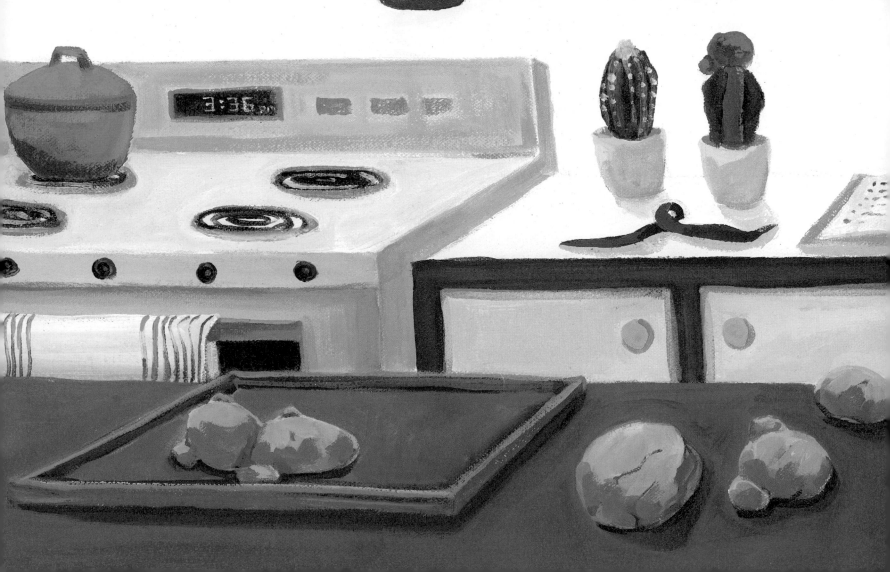

He tells me to go.

Home smells like warm bread.

"Surprise!" says Dad.

The sun sets.

Dad tucks.

Dad kisses.

Dad rests.

AUTHOR'S NOTE

AS A MURALIST, I consider myself lucky to work in places that most of us don't encounter in everyday life. I'm mostly talking about prisons and jails. I've worked in various correctional facilities, partnering on mural projects with people from different walks of life—mothers and teens, old and young, of every identity, belief system, and life experience.

Most often, the reasons for incarceration lie buried in layers of intergenerational trauma, untreated mental illness, institutionalized racism, poverty, and domestic violence. And within that entire tangled web, there are children. With each person I work with, I am struck by the devastating consequences of family separation. When a parent is incarcerated, they are not the only one who suffers. The loss of a mother or father to the system has a profound and lasting impact on families. Studies indicate that well over five million American children have experienced parental incarceration at one time or another, and some estimates are much higher. That is at least one in twelve children.

Every day, incarcerated mothers and fathers across the country parent their children with tremendous love and unbelievable resilience. Eventually, most people will return home to their families, to their communities. But the return is not easy due to the complex hardships related to the stigma of incarceration. Finding stable work is challenging. And the work of restorative healing, both from the trauma of incarceration and from whatever led to it—that can be the work of a lifetime.

I have encountered and collaborated with some incredible organizations devoted to rebuilding the lives of individuals and families after incarceration. Homeboy Industries in Los Angeles provides hope, training, and support to formerly gang-involved and incarcerated men and women, allowing them to redirect their lives and become contributing members of their communities. Detroit's On the Rise Bakery provides employment, supportive housing, training, counseling services, and educational opportunities. The Osborne Association provides a variety of services to those currently and formerly incarcerated, and to their children and families, and also leads a national initiative to support children whose parents are incarcerated called See Us, Support Us.

I am incredibly grateful for the opportunity to have partnered with several of these organizations, and for the essential work they do to make the world a better, more just place. All of these groups, as well as the ones listed below, inspired this book. All of the families impacted by incarceration who I've painted with through the years inspired this book. This book is for you.

LEARN MORE HERE:

Homeboy Industries, Los Angeles, CA: homeboyindustries.org

Hour Children, Long Island City, NY: www.hourchildren.org

On the Rise Bakery, Detroit, MI: www.cskdetroit.org/bakery

The Osborne Association, Brooklyn, NY: www.susu-osborne.org

STEPS to End Family Violence, New York, NY: www.risingground.org/program/steps

Women and Justice Project, Jackson Heights, NY: www.womenandjusticeproject.org